JAMES

PERCY

MEET ALL THESE FRIENDS IN BUZZ BOOKS:

The Animals of Farthing Wood
Thomas the Tank Engine
James Bond Junior
Fireman Sam
Joshua Jones
Blinky Bill
Rupert
Babar

First published 1990 by Buzz Books
an imprint of Reed Children's Books
Michelin House, 81 Fulham Rd, London SW3 6RB
and Auckland, Melbourne, Singapore and Toronto
Reprinted 1993

Photographs by David Mitton and Kenny McArthur
for Britt Allcroft's production of
Thomas the Tank Engine and Friends
ISBN 1 85591 006 3
Printed and bound in Italy by Olivotto

THOMAS DOWN THE MINE

One day Thomas was at the junction when Gordon shuffled in with some trucks.

"Poof!" said Thomas. "What a funny smell! Can you smell a smell?"

"I can't smell a smell," said Annie.

“It’s a funny, musty sort of smell,” said Thomas.

“No one noticed it until you did,” grunted Gordon. “It must be yours!” Not long ago Gordon had fallen into a dirty ditch. He knew that Thomas was teasing him about it.

"Annie and Clarabel, do you know what *I* think it is?" said Thomas. "It's ditchwater!" Gordon didn't have time to answer as Thomas was soon coupled to Annie and Clarabel and then he puffed quickly away.

Annie and Clarabel could hardly believe their ears. "He's *dreadfully* rude, I feel quite ashamed, I feel *quite* ashamed, he's dreadfully rude!" they twittered to each other.

They had great respect for Gordon, the big engine. "You mustn't be rude, you make us ashamed," they kept telling Thomas. But Thomas didn't care a bit.

"That was funny, that was funny," he chuckled, feeling very pleased with himself.

Thomas left the coaches at the station and went off to a mine for some trucks.

Long ago, miners digging for lead had made tunnels under the ground. The tunnel roofs were strong enough to hold trucks, but they could not take the weight of the heavy engines.

A large notice said: "DANGER ENGINES MUST NOT PASS THIS POINT"

Thomas had been warned but he didn't care. He had often tried to pass the sign before but had never succeeded. He knew the rules; he had to push empty trucks into one siding and wait to collect full ones from another.

1

This morning he laughed as he puffed along. He had made a plan. "Silly old board!" he said to himself, getting nearer and nearer to the danger sign.

The driver stopped him and the fireman went to turn the points. "Now for my plan," said Thomas and he bumped the trucks fiercely, jerking the driver off the footplate!

"Hurrah!" said Thomas, as he followed the trucks into a siding.

"Come back!" called his driver. But it was too late.

"Stupid old board!" said Thomas, as he ran past it. "There's no danger! There's no danger!"

“Look out!” cried the driver. The fireman clambered into the cab and tried Thomas’s brakes.

There was a rumbling noise and the rails quivered. The fireman jumped clear. Then the rails sagged and broke.

"Fire and smoke!" said Thomas. "I'm sunk!" – and he was! Thomas could just see out of the hole but he couldn't move. "Oh dear!" he said. "I *am* a silly engine."

"And a very naughty one, too," said the Fat Controller, who had just arrived. "I saw you."

"Please get me out. I won't be naughty again," said Thomas.

"I'm not sure," said the Fat Controller. "We can't lift you out with a crane because the ground is not firm enough. Hmm . . . let me see . . . I wonder if Gordon could pull you out."

"Yes, sir," said Thomas, nervously. He didn't want to see Gordon just yet.

When Gordon heard about Thomas he laughed very loudly. "Down a mine is he? Ho! Ho! Ho! What a joke! What a joke!" he chortled, puffing quickly to the rescue.

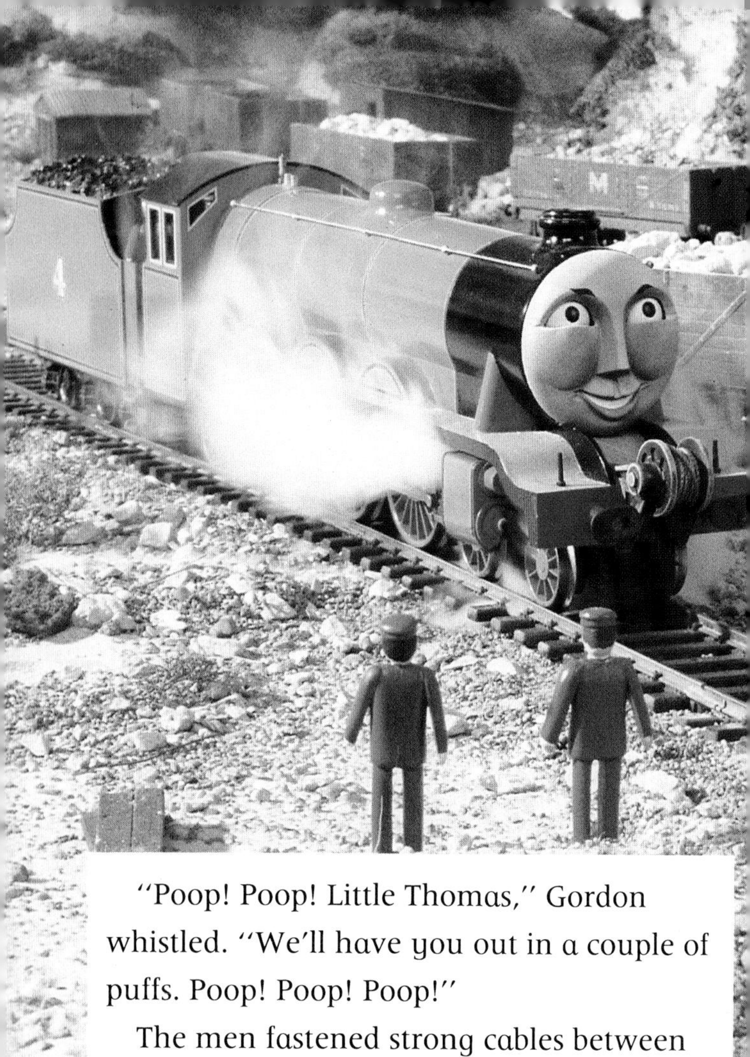

"Poop! Poop! Little Thomas," Gordon whistled. "We'll have you out in a couple of puffs. Poop! Poop! Poop!"

The men fastened strong cables between Gordon and Thomas.

1

"Are you ready? HEAVE!" called the Fat Controller.

But they didn't pull Thomas out in two puffs. It was a lot harder than they had all thought. Gordon worked hard but it took a long time to finally pull Thomas out of the hole.

1

"I'm sorry I was cheeky," said Thomas.

"That's all right, Thomas," said Gordon. "You made me laugh!" Thomas was very pleased that Gordon was not angry with him any more.

Thomas's fire had gone out so he needed a pull back to the station. "Can we go together?" asked Thomas.

"Of course we can," said Gordon. "I'll pull you back."

"Thank you very much," said Thomas. And buffer to buffer the two friends puffed home.

THOMAS
1

EDWARD
2

GORDON
4

One day Thomas was at the junction when Gordon shuffled in with some trucks.

"Poof!" said Thomas. "What a funny smell! Can you smell a smell?"

"I can't smell a smell," said Annie.

THOMAS DOWN THE MINE